D1238941

FINLAND

by Lee Kingman

pictures by Arnold Edwin Bare

Ariel Books – Farrar Straus and Cudahy

Not so long ago there lived a boy named Mikko. His blond hair was as bright as the sunshine, and his eyes were as blue as the lovely lakes in Finland where he lived.

Mikko was a brave boy, though he was only eight years old. For a long time his country was at war, and his father was a soldier. Mikko and his mother were very poor. They lived in a small cabin in the forest at the edge of a long lake, hoping someday Mikko's father would return.

Mikko loved the forest and the animals who lived in it. The birds and the deer and the squirrels were his friends.

He spent many hours in the summer talking and singing with them.

But summers in Finland, when the sky is light with sunshine almost all through the night, are very short. This year as winter came and the darkness crept out longer and longer, nibbling away at the daylight, Mikko knew that his mother was worried.

"What is the matter?" Mikko asked her one day, as they walked in the woods looking for mushrooms.

"We have put away potatoes and vegetables in the root cellar," said his mother. "But I wish we had a cow, and there is no money to buy one."

"A cow!" What a funny wish, Mikko thought. In the stories his mother told him, people often made wishes—but for something exciting. Not a cow! Mikko was not very fond of cows. They had to be milked, and they had strong minds of their own.

But Mikko loved his mother. She worked hard, and she wished for little. So Mikko found that he wished her wish, too. He wished they had a cow!

Next morning, Mikko said, "The best thing is to go to the big farm on the other side of the lake and see if they have a cow to sell. Perhaps I could work there and earn enough to buy a cow."

His mother smiled. "It would take a lot of work for a young boy to earn the price of a cow. But if you *think* you can do something, very often you can."

Mikko suddenly felt brave and strong. Almost as strong and brave as his father.

Then he remembered something. "Do you think there would be any money in Father's box?"

Mikko's mother looked at the wooden box, painted with worn but gay designs, where it stood under the window. "I know there isn't any money in it," she said sadly, "but when your father went away, he left you three gifts. Perhaps this is the time to give them to you."

From under her pillow she took a large key and gave it to Mikko. "Now you may open the chest, and you will see what they are."

Mikko was so excited.

He hoped there would be a hunting-knife in a leather case, and a pair of black shiny boots, and perhaps even a gun! Oh, the things he could do if he had those.

He turned the key and opened the chest. All his excitement blew away quicker than smoke!

There was a thick, worn book—a lantern—and a woolen scarf.

"Your father learned his A, B, C's from that book," Mother said, as he picked it up. "It was one of his most precious possessions."

"I know my A, B, C's," said Miko disgustedly. He put the book down with barely a glance. "And what kind of present is a lantern?"

"You never can tell when you may need the light of a lantern," his mother reminded him.

"Well, we can hang it on the peg by the doors," Mikko said rather crossly.

Then he took the scarf out of the chest. It was a beautiful one, knitted in gay colors.

"The pattern tells you one of the famous stories of the Kalevala," his mother said. "Here is Ilmarinen, strong and handsome, setting forth to win a beautiful maiden in the North country. He is riding on a sledge covered by a bearskin. A stallion is pulling the sledge, and on its yoke are six cuckoos, and there are seven blue birds singing on the reins."

Mikko looked carefully as his mother unfolded the scarf. It seemed to be very VERY VERY LONG.

"See, Mikko, here are the presents Ilmarinen took on his journey to give the maiden's mother. Here is the big bear of Tuoni, and the great wolf, and here is Tuoni's huge pike. Overhead flies the eagle who carried Ilmarinen on his back, and helped him subdue and capture the pike."

But Mikko was not impressed with the story of a young hero on a quest. He just looked at the whole great length of the scarf and began to laugh.

"How could I wear that without tripping on it?"

But as his mother hung it up carefully by the door, it made the wall look bright and gay, and she reminded Mikko, "This scarf tells a magic story.

Don't scorn your father's gifts, for there may be magic in them for you."

"Maybe," said Mikko. "But I don't see how."

He was greatly disappointed, but he kissed his mother good-bye, and set out through the forest to walk around the long lake to the farm and see about a cow.

Somehow, as he walked along, he couldn't help remembering the scarf and the story woven into it. He wished that he were as strong and handsome as the hero, and that he were going on a romantic adventure to find a beautiful maiden—not a cow. How sad it was that romantic adventures, full of wonder, never seemed to happen any more.

As Mikko went through the woods, he realized it was a beautiful day. The yellow birch leaves shook in soft little sounds of laughter, and the wind in the big pines was like the murmur of a happy heart.

The sparkle of the lake caught Mikko's eyes. When he came closer, he saw a boat near the shore. Perhaps as in the old stories, it carried a beautiful maiden who would turn into a swan if he spoke.

But it didn't. Mikko saw a rather pale little girl about his own age, and a

small boy with a round face, and an older boy who was pulling awkwardly on the oars and looked very cross.

Mikko hesitated. He saw that they were the children from the city who visited the farm in the summer. Perhaps if he called to them they would take him across the lake in the boat and save him a lot of steps and time.

"Hello!" Mikko called hopefully.

But the older boy suddenly made a great show of being able to row well, and sent the boat farther out into the lake.

So Mikko hiked all the way to the farm, and trudged all the way back. He came home just at dusk, tired, hungry, and without a cow.

"I saw cows, cows, and COWS!" Mikko groaned. "They are all new stock, a special herd. But there are none to spare and even if there were, the cost would be too great. I asked Mr. Pelto, the farm's owner, why just a simple cow was worth so much money—and he laughed."

"Don't feel so badly," said Mikko's mother. "You were brave and grown-up to go and talk to him."

"But he didn't think I was grown-up at all! He laughed, too, when I asked him for work. He said to come and play with his children. They are staying late this year because they have been sick."

"You should play more," said Mother with a sigh.

"I met them," Mikko said scornfully, "when they brought the boat in. Their names are Anna, Uno, and Timo. But we couldn't find anything to talk about."

It had not been a good day to seek a fortune or make friends.

"Never mind—you tried, and that's what counts. We'll forget the cow."

But Mikko could not forget the cow.

Each morning it was darker and colder. The sun rose later and seemed in a hurry to rush through the day as fast as it could.

The nights were long and frosty. Because Mikko lived too far from the village to go to school, he spent each day gathering brush, and doing his best to chop trees and split wood for the winter.

Every night his mother made the twigs and logs last as long as possible in the fireplace. The water in the pails was skimmed with ice in the morning.

One day as Mikko stepped outside to fetch more water, he knew it wouldn't be long before the whole lake would be frozen over.

If only they had a cow! How warm and friendly she would be. How good her milk would taste! Milking her would be a simple task, compared to chopping holes in the ice or melting snow for water.

The air was raw. The wind was sharp as a whip. When the sun rose, it looked as if it were frozen in ice.

Suddenly Mikko decided that today, before it was too late and they were snowed in for the winter, *HE WAS GOING TO GET A COW!*

That was all there was to it.

He tried on his winter cap. When his mother was busy cooking at the fireplace, he quietly lifted the lid of his father's box and slipped the book into his knapsack. If his father called it a precious possession, it might be valuable!

Perhaps he could sell it for the price of one cow—or maybe the price of one cow with a crumpled horn and a limp!

When he had eaten his breakfast, Mikko picked up his knapsack. As he stood in the doorway, he saw the knitted scarf and the lantern still hanging from pegs. If he took the book, he might as well take the other two things his father left him.

He wound the scarf around and around about his neck and over his head, and even around the waist of his coat.

"I feel like a top made out of wool!" Mikko laughed, as he spun the last length of the scarf over his shoulder.

"Just where are you going?" his mother asked.

"I'm going to seek our fortune," Mikko teased her. If he told her where he was going and why, she would worry about him all day. "I'll take the lantern, too, in case it is dark when I come home."

He put some long matches into his knapsack and kissed his mother good-bye.

“Be careful,” his mother said, “for even the air feels as if there were no good in it today.”

“I will,” Mikko promised.

He walked as fast as he could into the woods. The leaves had long left the trees, but their branches were slapping the wind. Even the big pines were bowing and groaning as if it hurt to bend.

Mikko was only halfway around the lake when he felt the first snowflake. Usually he was full of joy when the first snow fell, for he loved to ski. But now he began to worry how he could get a cow home through the snow—if he had a cow to bring home!

The wind began flinging the snowflakes wildly. They pricked and stung at his cheeks. Mikko could hardly see where he was going, for the storm was suddenly heavy and thick.

What was it his mother had said? You never could tell when you might need the light of a lantern.

Mikko stopped, and turning his back to the wind, struggled to light his lantern. It couldn't be a very magic gift from his father, for it was so hard to light. It might not even help him to see, but at least it would make him feel as if he wasn't quite so alone. Finally the light caught.

No sooner did the light flare out than Mikko heard shouts from the lake. "Help! Help! We are lost!"

Mikko held the lantern high and looked all around. There, perched one minute on top of an angry gray wave, and the next minute shoved out of sight, was a rowboat. In it were the frightened children from the farm. It was Anna,

the girl, who was screaming in a high thin voice. The small boy, Timo, had covered his face with his hands. Uno, the older one, hung frantically to the oars.

"Here! Come here!" cried Mikko, waving his lantern. "Here is the shore!"

While he watched the violent waves whipped by the wind, he wondered

if the boy rowing would be strong enough to pull to shore. "If you have a rope, throw it to me!" he called, putting down the lantern.

Anna, though she was weeping hard, found the rope and threw it as far as she could. But it fell short. Had she kept hold of the other end?

The boat dipped out of sight, and the snow stung his eyes. Mikko blinked and winked. There the boat was once more, and Anna was pulling the rope back, ready to throw again. This time the boat lurched, and when she threw the rope with all her might, she almost fell out of the boat.

Mikko jumped high into the air, and this time he caught the rope and hauled as hard as he could. At last the boat grated on the shore.

"Oh, thank you! Thank you!" cried Anna, tumbling out of the boat.

Little Timo was crying so hard he couldn't talk. Mikko felt sorry for him, but the older boy, Uno, should have known better than to go rowing on a day like this. Surely even visiting children from the city would know better.

"What were you doing out on the lake on a day like this?" Mikko asked.

"We just wanted to go once more before the lake was frozen," said Anna.

"And the storm came up so quickly," explained Uno.

"I want to go home," wailed Timo.

"I will show you," said Mikko. "I will light the way with my lantern."

So they started out with the snow and wind beating about them. But not very far along, Timo began to cry louder than ever.

"I can't see a thing. I can't see where I'm going."

Mikko had an idea. He stopped and put down the lantern. Then he began to unwind the long knitted scarf. He spun himself around and around until he was dizzy, but at last it was off.

"Here," said Mikko. He took one end and tied it tight around Timo's waist. Then he made Anna stand ahead of Timo and looped the scarf around her, and a little ahead of her, he put a loop around Uno. The other end he tied to his own waist. There they all were, roped together like mountain climbers

—and Timo at last stopped howling. Wasn't it lucky that his father's scarf was so very long!

When Mikko finally led the children in at the gate of the farm, Mr. Pelto was just on his way to search for them. In the doorway, their mother was waiting and watching anxiously.

"Here they are, sir!" called Mikko, waving his lantern.

"Here we are!" cried Anna. "This boy saved us."

How Mr. Pelto hugged the children! Their mother ran out to touch them and make sure they were real. Mikko tried to step out of the way of their joyful meeting, but he had forgotten they were all tied together with the scarf. He almost tripped himself right upside down.

Mikko began to untie it, when Mr. Pelto cried, "Look at this!" He made the children stand in line, so everyone who had come running out, could see how Mikko had brought them home.

"You are a resourceful boy," he said. "But what are you doing so far from your home in a storm like this?"

"It wasn't storming when I started," Mikko said—and realized that was just what Uno had told him. He suddenly looked at Uno and the two boys grinned at each other. "I was setting out to seek my fortune."

He hadn't meant to say that—it sounded so foolish. But it just slipped out.

"To seek your fortune!" Anna and Timo and Uno stared at Mikko in surprise. They had never met anyone before who was on his way to seek a fortune.

"Well," Mikko said, and blushed, "really I'm on my way to find a cow for my mother. I have a book to sell in the village, and I hope it will bring enough to buy a cow."

"Come inside, Mikko," said Mr. Pelto, "and warm up by the fire. Perhaps you would show me the book."

Mikko blew out the lantern, and laughingly they all unwound themselves from the scarf.

By the kitchen fire, Mikko shook out the scarf, and started to fold it and put it into his knapsack.

"What a beautiful scarf!" said Mrs. Pelto. "Do let me see every bit of it."

Mikko spread it out on the table. "When my father went away to be a soldier, he left me three things—a scarf, a lantern, and a book. I didn't think very much of them at first. I really wanted a gun, some boots, and a knife. But the scarf and the lantern were suddenly very useful, and if I can sell the book—"

"Let me see it, Mikko," Mr. Pelto said.

Mikko took it out. If only it were valuable! If only Mr. Pelto would buy

it, and if only it would be enough for a cow. Mikko handed him the book, and as he did so, he felt suddenly sad, for it was one of the three things his father had left him.

But Mr. Pelto did not seem interested at all in the book. He merely glanced at it, and handed it back to Mikko.

Mikko's hopes began to sink. Mr. Pelto put a kind hand on his shoulder. "The book is not worth money, but it will be valuable to you when you are older because of the many wise thoughts in it. Your father was right to leave it to you, and you should keep it for your son someday. A scarf, and a lantern and a book may not be what you wanted, but in their way, they are great gifts. What you should realize, Mikko, is that you have given *me* a great gift."

Mikko stared in surprise. How had he given a gift when he had nothing to give?

"You gave me back my three children," the farmer said. "What would they have done if they hadn't seen the light of your lantern on the shore, or if you hadn't known the way and led them so safely? Come with me, Mikko, and we shall pick out a present to express my thanks."

Mikko hardly dared hope as he and Anna, Uno, and Timo and Mr. Pelto

went out into the yard. But Mr. Pelto was leading them to the barn!

"Here are my prize cows, Mikko," he said, and Mikko saw that if you could really call a cow beautiful, these were very beautiful indeed. No wonder the farmer did not want to sell one for a book, a scarf, and a lantern.

But what was he saying? Mikko could hardly believe his ears. He had to wait until Mr. Pelto said it again.

"You may choose any one you like to take home to your mother."

Mikko felt such a burst of joy he could hardly say thank you. He walked slowly up and down. The cows all looked so sturdy and so calm. At last he chose one that seemed to look a little more friendly than the others.

Even during the delicious dinner in the warm kitchen, Mikko was eager to be on his way home and show his mother the cow.

"Stay and play with us for a while," Uno begged.

"I'll come another day," Mikko promised. "On my skis."

Going out, he found the storm had cleared. The sun burst forth, and every corner of the sky and snow-covered earth sparkled and shone.

Mr. Pelto brought out the cow, and was going to fetch a rope for her. But Mikko took his scarf and wound it around her neck. Gently, he led her out of the yard, and turned to wave his unlit lantern at his new friends.

Along the lake, they plodded, going slowly, for the sake of the swaying

cow. It was soon dark, and Mikko was grateful once more for the lantern before he came to the cabin in the woods.

His mother was waiting anxiously for him. "So you went to seek your fortune! And where is it?"

"Right here! Just as in the Kalevala, I've brought home a beautiful maiden."

Mikko opened the door wide, and pulled the scarf until the astonished cow was right inside the cabin.

His mother was so surprised she couldn't say anything but "A cow! A cow!" over and over.

"Not just a cow," said Mikko proudly. After all, she was a special cow. She deserved a special name.

While his mother patted and admired the cow, Mikko thoughtfully put the wise book back in the chest, and hung up the helpful lantern and the wonderful scarf. His father had left him three fine gifts after all. They had certainly helped him to seek his fortune, and he had found it.

Why of course. That was it!

"Not just a cow, Mother," Mikko said. "Her name is Fortune."